For Rita, Henry, Edward, Luca & Marcus.

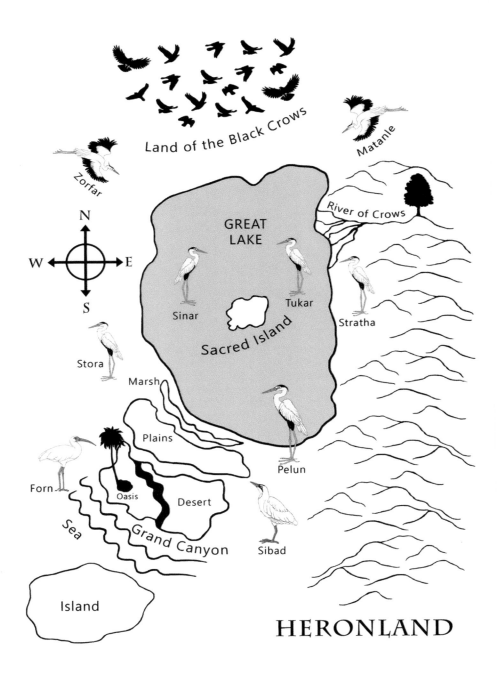

Land of the Black Crows

Matanle

Zorfar

River of Crows

N

W   E

S

GREAT
LAKE

Sinar

Tukar

Stratha

Stora

Sacred Island

Marsh

Plains

Pelun

Forn

Oasis

Desert

Sibad

Sea

Grand Canyon

Island

HERONLAND

PROLOGUE: THE COLD WIND

A cold wind has been blowing from the North for many months now and I can feel the evil upon it. The Invaders are on the move again.

I am Pelun, the head of the Southern flocks of Great Heron families that form part of the Heron nation. For countless seasons, we have all lived happily in a pleasant climate around the shores of Great Lake.

The vast expanse of Great Lake stretches as far as the eye can see. It holds an abundance of fish which we hunt and is fringed with green reed beds and many trees that provide safe havens for our nursery nests.

My grandparents brought me here as a young fledgling, a journey that I scarcely remember. They told me that both my parents had died defending their flock against the Invaders that came from the North. Now it seems that it is to be my turn to protect my flock.

A strange Stork had brought the warning that the Invaders – the Black Crows – were making preparations to attack the Heron Nation and that they were a dangerous threat to our future. As a result, an emergency meeting of our Council has been called and I must fly there immediately.

CHAPTER I
THE COUNCIL

CHAPTER I

THE COUNCIL

The evening sun was sinking and the darkening sky was studded with stars and lit by a rising full moon as I crossed beaks with my lifetime companion Rosandris to bid her farewell.

As I rose up into the sky, circling our territory, I thought about how we'd brought up our children in this place and my heart swelled with pride. Now they have their own partners and we all live together as one extended family.

I flew higher and followed the soft, shimmering silver moonbeam that seemed to lead across the lake to the as yet unseen Sacred Island in the far distance.

This small, circular isle, situated equidistant from all the shores of Great Lake, was inhabited by the all-white Kotakin Herons, a rare breed who, since time immemorial, have served as spiritual leaders and peacemakers for our nation.

It was neutral ground where both the heads of the Great Heron flocks that make up our nation and family elders could meet in peace. There were always petty differences and squabbles between flocks and families and fights frequently broke out.

If these disputes couldn't be resolved, then they'd be brought before the Council at their regular full moon meetings when the Great Herons' leaders, elected by their flocks, came to discuss their collective problems.

These meetings were presided over by two of the Kotakin herons - Senar and Tukar – the priests who passed judgment according to the Laws of the Flock that all Herons had to obey. Their authority was symbolized by the Council's totem, a large white sacred plume.

At the last moon meet, we'd been sitting on old reed nests in a traditional circle when Mantanle and Zorfar - two of the youngest of the Council Members and joint leaders of the Northern Flocks - arrived bringing with them a stranger. They begged us to hear him.

The Stork looked tired and haggard as he bowed to us all. As was the custom, the sacred plume was passed to him to allow him the authority to speak to the Council.

"I bring you grave warnings about the Black Crows", he said. "They have caused havoc amongst my flocks and they are planning to bring chaos to your peaceful nation."

This news sent a ripple of unease around the circle and everyone leaned forward closer so as not to miss the details of the Stork's story.

"Twenty moons ago, a large colony of us were living peacefully in a forest far from here when, one day, we saw in the sky a huge, black cloud. At first we thought it was a signal of the onset of an early winter. However, as the cloud came closer and closer, we could see that it was made up of thousands and thousands of Black Crows.

"They descended, without warning, on our nests and showed no mercy towards us, killing old and young, male and female. Their fierce cries haunt me still. The women and children watched in tearful terror as they saw their menfolk and sons surrounded by the Invaders in a fight to the death. Their turn came next."

"After fighting for hours, I alone managed to outrun the last few of the Crows who had tried to bring me down. I have been a wanderer ever since. I have flown here to warn you. Do not suffer our fate. You must flee before it is too late to save yourselves!"

Having delivered his warning, the Stork bowed low and flew off into the night sky.

Matanle and Zorfar once more urged us to take heed of this warning so the Council decided to call an emergency meeting.

*

After a long flight, as I got closer to the island, the sky was full of what looked like at least a hundred birds, not only Great and Grey Herons but also some Bitterns who were our allies.

When we had all landed and settled ourselves I looked around, I saw that all the main flocks and families were represented. There was Matanle and Zorfar, our greatest warrior, with a number of their followers, who led the Northern flocks. Stratha, the head of the Eastern region, also came with followers. The West was represented by the female figure of Stora. I was the sole representative of the Southern flocks.

In an outer ring sat the lesser chiefs who watched as Zorfar stood up and stepped into the middle of the circle. He related the details of the dreadful fate that had befallen the Stork's flock and the warnings he had given. His words were met by a numb silence and a look of fear spread across the faces of the assembled. All eyes turned towards the centre as Senar stood up and took the floor.

"We are a nation with a sacred spirit which we hold dear. When we die we pass on to the spirit in the skies. Our code of values and laws, passed down to us from time immemorial, celebrate peace, freedom of the individual and the responsibility of the flock towards the nation.

"We have a Council elected by all and a sect of priests who help run the Council and send out emissaries to minister to each flock. All this is threatened by the tyrannical regime of the Black Crows. We have received a timely warning. What should we do?"

Matanle was the first to speak. "I believe we should fight. We are a large nation. We have thousands of young Herons well trained in hunting. Surely we can see off this threat!" Others, including Zorfar, nodded in agreement.

Then Stora spoke up. "If the Black Crows come this way and are as numerous as we are led to believe, we will surely be outnumbered and our families will be defenceless against them."

The arguments raged between those who wanted to flee and those who wanted to stay and fight. Senar raised his voice and spoke up above the rest. "Let us ask Pelun. He is one of the wisest of us. His judgments have served us well in the past."

There was a murmur of approval and a hush fell over the Council. I spoke loudly and clearly so everyone could hear.

"We must do both things my wise friends have spoken of. Matanle and Zorfar should prepare to fight. They should gather together their young warriors and prepare them for battle while also scouts are sent to the far Northern borders ready to sound the alarm if they see the Black Crows arriving."

There was a further murmur of approval from some of the members but when I raised my voice again and said "We should also leave the Lake" everyone gasped in surprise.

"We should prepare a great evacuation. All the flocks should send their women and young away to the West for, if the Crows are as numerous as we hear, then even with our brave fighters, we will not stand a chance. It is better to prepare for both eventualities. The fighters that survive can follow on and protect us. Only in this way can we ensure the survival of our great nation."

A huge clamour broke out and arguments raged backwards and forwards amongst the members. Several of the female leaders had tears in their eyes and some of the older heads shook their beaks in disbelief and anger.

Senar called the meeting to order and spoke: "Pelun is right. It is the only way to ensure survival. Let us vote." One by one, each Heron bent their head and touched the floor, signifying their approval. Then all heads turned towards me again.

"I have given a great deal of thought as to who should go where and when. We cannot escape to the North, home of the Black Crows. We cannot go far to the South or East because of the great mountain ranges. We still don't know what lies beyond them. So we must go West, over plains, desert and sea until we reach the Island our legend speaks of. Then we will be safe."

Fear came into the eyes of everyone. Tukar, the fellow priest who helped Senar, spoke up:
 "We know the Island exists but we know little of it. No one from our flocks has recently ventured that far. How can we be sure that we will not perish and starve or be driven by gales into the sea. We are not sea birds. We need land to perch on. We need rivers, banks and fish from fresh water."

This speech was met by worried murmurs all around the Council.

Senar called the assembly to order. "We must vote again to decide on Pelun's plan." One by one the beaks were lowered. Some responded immediately while others, with some trepidation, bowed only after seeing which way the others voted. Only one or two beaks were raised against it. My plan was passed.

Then I noticed that neither Matanle or Zorfar had voted. They were skulking together at the back of the circle talking amongst their followers. When they noticed I was watching them, they both came into the circle and lowered their beaks like the others. They avoided looking at me directly.

"We are grateful to Pelun, the Great Heron, for his wise counsel" Senar said. "We have decided to allow Matanle and Zorfar to gather the War Flocks to defend us in the North. Stratha leading the flocks from the East will rendezvous with the Southern herons to fly across Great Lake to where they will join together with Stora and her flocks in the West.

"Go and break the news to your loved ones," he added, "You must all be ready to leave as soon as possible. Tukar and I will remain here on the Sacred Island and be the last to leave. May the spirit be with you"

Everyone bowed to Senar and Tukar and then gradually dispersed, some full of silent thoughts, others chattering noisily. One by one we all flew off and away into the clear night sky to prepare for our tasks and the journey ahead.

CHAPTER II
EXODUS

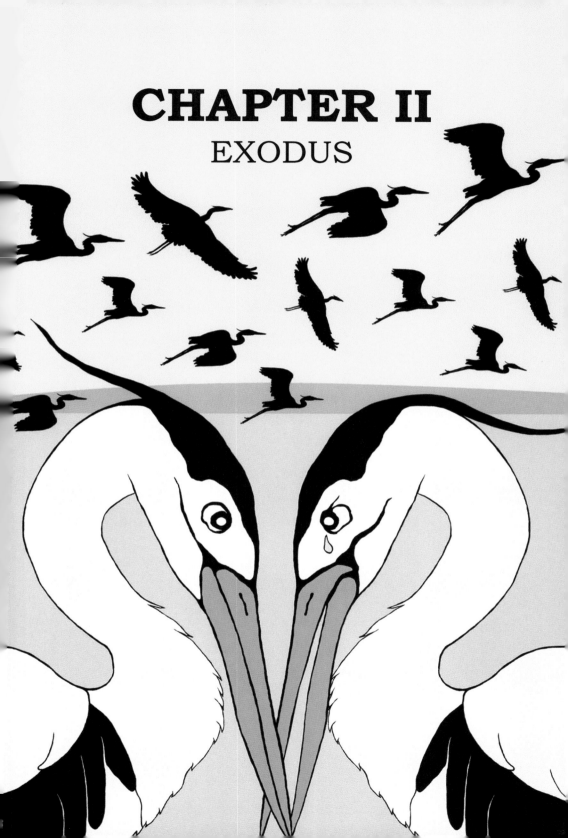

CHAPTER II

EXODUS

The first finger of sunlight pointed across Great Lake as I flew low over the glistening water. All was still and calm. It was hard to believe that this tranquil place, our home, was to be abandoned.

Throughout my life, I'd been haunted by my grandfather's tales of the last time they had attacked us. On his deathbed he told me "Beware the Black Crows. They are controlled by a creed which is alien to us Great Herons. They will not tolerate any dissent from their way of life. They will destroy any creature that gets in their way." Now the Crows are on the move again.

Ahead of me I could now see the shoreline fringed with thick bulrushes and squat trees full of scattered nests and the morning sounds of the awakening flock.

I alighted on my nest in the midst of the heronry where my Rosandris was there waiting faithfully for me. Our beaks met in a loving caress and she looked deep into my eyes.

"It is as expected," I said. A tear ran down her cheek. "We must prepare our departure my love but now I must sleep."

Breaking the news the following morning to my own family and the rest of the flock was not easy but once they understood the mortal danger facing all of them, even the younger children, understood the need to take flight.

*

Preparations for the journey were made in haste. I explained they could take nothing with them. All were encouraged to gather food and eat heartily in order to sustain themselves through the long flight.

First we selected one hundred of the youngest and fittest male and female herons who were commanded to join the warriors assembled by Matanle and Zorfar in the North.

They were to be led by Fedele, my youngest son. He was, like me at his age, strong of wing, bold, but also a good thinker who would serve our cause well.

I instructed him carefully about how to divide the birds into three flights - the swiftest to fly in front, the strongest to fly at the rear and, on both sides of the flock, those with the keenest of eyes scanning the sky for trouble. It was prearranged that they were to fly along the shores, meeting up with warrior birds from other flocks, to join the forces of the North.

Once assembled, our young warriors dipped their beaks silently together as I, as head of the flock, blessed them. They said their farewells to friends and family before rising into the steadily darkening sky. It was now time to prepare the rest of the flock.

I chose my eldest son Pulla to lead the flight and hook up with Stora. He, along with all the males of the flock, were instructed to form a huge outer defense ring to protect the inner flock of mothers and daughters who would, in turn protect the fledglings. At the rear some of the older and strongest herons, were stationed so, if someone faltered, they could be supported until they were strong enough to rejoin the flock.

There was to be silence en route, so they practiced the signs and wing beats that would enable them to communicate with each other.

As far as possible, the flocks were to try and travel at night, navigating by the moon and stars, and hide and rest during the day. Advance parties would scout ahead for suitable sites.

All was nearing completion and it was time for me to leave the flock. I had another role to fulfill.

It was not easy saying goodbye to Rosandris. We had been together for a long time. I first saw her stretching her lovely neck on the banks of the water not far from where we had settled.

She looked lovingly at me as I told her that I had a mission to undertake and that I would see her on the Western shore if all went well. She had always understood my sense of duty and the important role that I was playing in this great undertaking. This time round, both our sons were also involved.

My task had been agreed secretly with Senar and Tukar after the emergency Council Meeting. It was to ensure that all the Council's commands were carried out correctly.

I was to fly North to await the arrival of the Black Crows and observe how Matanle and Zorfar were faring with their defence. If all was well, I was to fly back to report to Senar at the Sacred Isle.

Senar was worried. "Old friend" he said, "The warning we have received is strange. I do not doubt that the Stork was sincere and that he had clearly suffered but, when I tried at the last meeting to question him, Matanle and Zorfar insisted on being present. It made me uneasy. I don't know who the Stork was more scared of - the Black Crows or Matanle" I shared his disquiet. I had also found Matanle and Zorfar's reactions rather strange.

*

Senar had appointed a companion for the flight North namely Sibad, the astute leader of the Bitterns. I'd had many conversations at Council meetings with him in the past and he'd become a trusted ally and friend. I was pleased to have some company for the task ahead.

The Bitterns were related to us Great Herons and their families and our flocks had once lived side by side on the shores of Great Lake. However, many moons ago, most of them left to find their own waters far to the North. The few families that remained were in service to the Council on the Island.

By the time I arrived back there Sibad was waiting for me in the island's reeds and flew up to meet me. We greeted each other warmly and, without more ado, turned to the North, flying swiftly into the darkening night.

Many hours later, Sibad suddenly swooped down and gestured for me to follow. We had reached the eastern shore and were flying across reed beds and woods that stretched a little way inland. Nearby grasslands were punctuated by a slow-moving river that formed a delta as it flowed into Great Lake. Further inland we caught a glimpse of a distant mountain range.

Alighting in the woods, we settled down to sleep for a few hours. I dropped off as soon as I closed my eyes and woke with a start from a dream in which Black Crows were tumbling out of the skies. Sibad was already awake and, within a short time, we were flying off into the wakening landscape, heading towards the mountains in the distance.

As the day wore on and we got closer we could see that one of the highest peaks was crowned by a giant tree. Sibad's plan was to use this as our lookout post. From there, we should be able to see as far as the northern tip of Great Lake. By the end of the day we reached this mighty wonder of nature and settled down for the night, hoping to make an early start at first light the following morning.

When we awoke a vast landscape was spread out in front of our eyes. As we scanned the horizon there was one unusual sight on the horizon. It appeared to be a huge churning cloud. As the day progressed and the cloud got nearer we suddenly realised it was composed of the Heron Nation's warriors - thousands of them, in formation, at various levels in the sky, practicing their battle formations. Our hearts swelled with pride. This huge army was our front-line defence against the Crows.

Great Lake could be seen glimmering to our left. We looked right towards the far Eastern horizon but there was nothing in sight. It was completely clear of any sign of the Crows. We'd carried out our orders as planned.

CHAPTER III
THE INVASION

CHAPTER III

THE INVASION

As the light brightened we started to make ready to leave when Sibad suddenly gasped and gestured to me to look down. At the foot of the mountain there appeared to be a dark river which the sun had yet to illuminate. Something was wrong.

To our horror, we both realised that, what at first had appeared to be the currents and waves of the river, was in fact a multitude of Black Crows.

Our warriors were looking for the Black Crows in the far North but the Crows were, in fact, heading in a different direction. Using the cliffs as cover, they were following the course of the river and were now massing for an invasion of the Great Lake. If that happened, the great flocks gathering for the journey Westwards would be very vulnerable without the Warriors. We have to alert them somehow.

The sun rose ever higher and we noticed a small flight of spotter crows heading in our direction. We hastily dropped to the ground and hid in the shadow of a big boulder as they flew overhead. We could now see other Crows scanning the landscape. It was only a matter of time before our presence would be revealed.

We conferred in our lowest tones and agreed that we have to try and force the Crows to fly upwards to alert the Warriors to their existence. That's when we noticed that the boulder we were sheltering behind was actually quite precariously perched on the edge of small slope which the weather had eroded.

We began furiously clearing as much of the smaller boulders and rocks beneath it. By the time we'd cleared a path, the boulder was already unstable. A large limb that had fallen from the tree nearby provided a strong lever. Using all my strength I managed to use it to shift the rock just enough to dislodge it from its crumbling base. As it started to roll, it gained momentum, loosening a torrent of rocks and stones and unhinging a giant fractured piece of the cliff which fell with a huge roar into the gorge below creating pandemonium among the Crows. The dusty air was filled with the deafening screams and frightened sounds of dying and injured birds.

We used the confusion to make our escape, turning North and flying as hard as we could. After what seemed like hours, we caught our first glimpse of the Heron warriors on the far horizon. They were heading back in our direction having, we later discovered, been alerted by their own high-flying scouts who patrolled the skies in case of attacks from behind.

As the great army flew into closer view a thousand-strong battle group of elite flyers peeled off from the main flock and formed themselves into a flying V. This was the advanced guard of the swiftest Herons.

At that point, I looked for Sibad and realized he had dropped behind me, was flying slowly and looking shaky. I flew towards him and saw he was bleeding from the beak and wing, injuries probably caused by falling debris.

I glanced back again and caught sight of great waves of Crows in the distance. We could hear their rallying calls. They were organizing their counter-attack and preparing to fight. We were caught between the two forces.

As a Great Heron, I'd trained to be a warrior in my youth. When I became a Champion I survived many contests and challenges. This was going to be a great battle which I should, by rights, be a part of but my highest imperative had to be to follow orders and report back to Senar this dramatic state of affairs.

Sibad was in no fit state to fight and needed care. I floated underneath him, and gradually flew up until he was resting upon my back. He wasn't heavy and I could still fly without problems. I swiftly swooped down and away from the confrontation until we could clearly see the trees and swamps where we would be able to rest and hide.

My plan then was to make our way slowly on a parallel track to the river until we reached Great Lake. From there, we could fly to the Council's Sacred Island first and deliver our message before flying on to the Western shores of the lake where the rest of the Heron Nation would already be gathered.

Once we'd travelled a safe distance, I settled us both down in a tree and turned to watch the two armies engage.

The advance flight, which had the two Giant Heron commanders Matanle and Zorfar at its head and a substantial flock of warriors behind, was closing in on the Crows. The surviving Black Crows had formed themselves into a long black line awaiting the attack.

Something was wrong! Matanle, Zorfar and the advance party had reached the Crows but instead of fighting a battle, the Crows parted to allow the two commanders to fly through their midst unharmed and come out the other side, where they just hung in the air currents as if they were spectators.

The solid mass of Crows was as thick as a forest, blocking out the sun's rays so that the ground was shadowed. They closed in on the warriors of the advanced flight.

The Crows and the Herons clashed. Great waves of fighting birds filled the skies. It seemed like thousands of Crows were being torn apart but their numbers never seemed to diminish. There were just too many. We were being overwhelmed. The cries filled the air as they plunged into battle, the screeching of the Herons mingling with the croaking of the Crows.

Suddenly the cries were overtaken by the deep resonant sound of the Herons' retreat call. The survivors were disengaging, regrouping and protecting their injured and each other as they staged a tactical withdrawal.

The Crows let out a huge cry, beating their wings in triumph, swooping through the skies, wave after wave, jubilant at their victory. Matanle could be seen at their front, clearly in command but of Zorfar there was no sign. Gradually they calmed down, regrouped and resumed their journey following the river to Great Lake.

It was time for us to go. Our suspicions about Matanle and Zorfar had been correct. They were traitors to our nation.

Sibad's wounds had stopped bleeding and he'd regained some of his energy so we carefully and slowly picked our way through the trees. I didn't have time to dwell on my anger at their betrayal. We were going to have to be careful and fly only at night if we were to avoid the crows.

Three days later we reached the shores of Great Lake. Sibad looked well fed and rested and seemed capable of flying under his own power. As night came on, we lifted off into the chill air heading for the Island.

My mind was full of dark thoughts. I knew Senar had suspicions about Matanle and Zorfar so news of their treachery may not come as a great surprise. The Black Crows' new tactics will be a shock. Our mission could not be more important. The survival of our entire Heron Nation was now in the balance.

CHAPTER IV
THE ISLAND

CHAPTER IV

THE ISLAND

Clouds covered Great Lake, obscuring the moonlight. We'd been flying for most of the night and were now not far away from the Island.

We would soon be able to warn Senar about the threat of the Black Crows. We'd witnessed the first battle with their great army. The shrewd withdrawal of our Northern flock, under the leadership of my youngest son, Fedele means we have the resources, to fight again.

If the Council's plans have been followed correctly, the main flock should already be on their way inland from the great gathering place on the Western shore.

One thing was certain. We needed to try and find out what Matanle and Zorfar were planning to do next. They have forged some kind of alliance with the Black Crows and betrayed us for their own ends.

I glanced over at Sibad who, despite being injured, was bravely flying beside me. On the horizon, as dawn was breaking, we could see the shores of our Sacred Isle appearing.

Sibad drew back, took a sharp turn to the right and gestured to me to follow him. Circling around the Isle we headed for a small stream with reeds on either side that would provide good cover. We flew upstream, following its winding course which led us to the familiar Council circle. We landed and walked towards its centre.

Strangely there were no guards. Normally there were always one or two of Sibad's Bitterns on duty to serve Senar and the Council. I glanced at Sibad and could see he was worried. He said: "You must hide now. Something is wrong. I will find out".

He scurried away into the undergrowth. I looked up at the trees and saw a round circle of nests. They were all empty and it looked as if they may have been abandoned in haste as the ground below was scattered with twigs and branches.

Sibad returned with Cathe, a fellow Bittern who I recognised from Council Meetings. He was a sorry sight with his torn cloak and dishevelled feathers He spoke at Sibad's bidding:

"It was the Black Crows. Thousands of them descended from the East in a great cloud. We stood no chance.

"I was lucky. I had just returned to report that the great exodus from the Western shores led by Stora was well under way, when I saw the Black Crows descending. I hid and saw what happened." He broke down and Sibad put a comforting wing around him. "Go on," he said. "Tell Pelun."

Cathe sobbed "I saw Senar and Tukar back to back in the centre of the Council Circle, fighting beak and claw with the Crows. It was too much. They were overwhelmed. They and a number of their attendants sacrificed themselves to distract the Crows whilst their families escaped."

"Tell him what you saw then" said Sibad. I glanced at him reproachfully. Clearly, Cathe had had a terrible experience. Sibad shook his head. "It just get's worse" he said.

Cathe took a deep breath. "It was Zorfar. He had led the Black Crows here. He was the only one who would have known the route. Zorfar was standing on one of the nests, looking at the Black Crows attacking Senar.

"When Senar saw him he let out a great screech, broke free and tried to reach him. A dozen Crows who were protecting Zorfar, rose up and cut and tore Senar to pieces".

I grabbed Cathe. "Where did Zorfar go?"

"I don't know. I hid. I was too scared that they would attack me. I hid until I was found by Sibad."

The only thought in my mind was that the traitors Matanle and Zorfar must be stopped at all costs. I knew what to do.

"Sibad, we have to get word to Fedele in the North. You and Cathe must tell him what has happened. Instruct him to summon his remaining warriors to join us and cover the exodus.

"The Black Crows will probably by now know of the flocks' departure. They will be gathering to pursue them. I will fly to the West to meet the rearguard and rally them. You and Cathe must find the Warriors at all costs and get them to meet me."

I plucked out one of my distinctive wing feathers for Sibad to take to Fedele. "This will verify that your message comes from me. Fly now, as quickly as you can and tell them to hurry but to be careful."

Sibad bowed to me and took the wing feather. He and Cathe took off as night fell. I watched them fly low across the lake heading North, keeping far away from the shores where the Crows would be patrolling. I wished them well.

I had one last duty to perform. I returned to the circle of nests. Cathe had said that when Senar was killed he was not wearing his Leader's badge of office - The White Heron's feather known as the Sacred Plume. He must have hidden it and only I knew where it was. Looking at the state of the other nests, it was clear that Zorfar had tried to find it but without success.

I found the special nest intact and there, in the secret cavity that Senar had shown me many moons ago, was what I was looking for - the pure white feather, symbol of our nation. I tucked it deep into my plumage. I will now have to assume the supreme guardianship of our Council and Nation. I'm ready for the task.

CHAPTER V
THE CHASE

CHAPTER V

THE CHASE

It was another cloudy night as I sped low across the water heading for the Western shore. I did not feel at all tired. My mind was in turmoil.

It seemed such a long time ago that I had said goodbye to my beloved Rosandris and made my way to the North. I had witnessed the first battle with the Black Crows, the treachery of Matanle and Zorfar and learned of the destruction of our beloved Council Leaders. My blood boiled at the thought of it all.

We are not a vengeful nation. We are easy-going and freedom-loving but, if threatened, we feel justified in defending our flocks. We had no choice but to flee from the Black Crows. What really filled me with anger was the fact that two of our own kind had betrayed us. As I flew on through the night my anger ebbed away. I knew that in these matters a hot head does not help. To win the war I must remain calm, centre myself and think clearly about the problems ahead.

As the dawn was just beginning to light up the distant sky, I redoubled my wing beats and swooped down. Catching first sight of the Western shore where I should be safe and able to rest amongst the trees and reeds.

Then I noticed that a group of Black Crows had flown up above the trees and were circling each other in animated discussion as if they had just woken. I shuddered to think what would happen if they caught me before I could warn the main flock. I might be able to out run them but not for long.

Flying lower still, the brightening sunlight made me much more visible. Sure enough, one of the crows set off a chorus of croaks and the excited birds headed in my direction. I had been spotted.

I reached the shore, and hopped into a flourishing reed bed, making sure not to damage the bulrushes. Deep in this thicket, I tucked my head under my wings, knelt down, made myself as invisible as possible and waited.

It didn't take long before I heard the flutter of wings and the cries of the Crows overhead. They flew in sweeping circles, getting more and more frustrated as they couldn't spot me.

Then came a different but familiar sound - the steady beat of Herons' wings. Was this a flock coming to my rescue. Was I saved?

Then, in a flash, I realized it was Zorfar and his Heron lieutenants. He was issuing commands to the Black Crows to search the reeds more thoroughly.

What was I to do? It was a long time until nightfall. Should I stay here hidden and risk being discovered or try and make my escape now? I pushed my beak under my breast to check that the Sacred Plume was still there. Its presence filled me with strength and confidence.

The rustling noise of the Crows pushing their way through the reeds was getting closer. I raised my head to see that some crows above me had now been joined by three herons. They spotted my sudden movement and now there was no escape.

I lifted myself up, puffed up my chest and let out the war cry of the Great Herons. This disconcerted them for a moment and I flew straight out and up to attack the lead warrior, a young one who I could see had recognized my eminence with a swift nod of the head. The other two herons hung back, waiting to see the outcome.

It was over very quickly. He came straight for me at speed. I swiftly sidelined his charge and bloodied his head with my sharp beak. Before he could recover, I swung underneath him and carved a long bloody line on his underside then caught one of his wings with my talons and heard it snap. He gave out a loud screech as he tumbled to the ground. The other Herons turned tail.

Then I was off and away as fast as my wings could carry me. It was a long time since I had taken a life but I had little choice. I knew I could outrun the Crows and, sure enough, the chaos of calls faded rapidly behind me. Luck was with me. Zorfar's advance party was certain to wait for the great flock of crows to arrive. I must now fly like the wind to alert the Heron flock.

CHAPTER VI

THE SEARCH

CHAPTER VI

THE SEARCH

Resting by day and flying by night, I made my way in haste to the point on the Western shore where a belt of marshland, with its maze of streams, extends from the Lake. This was a famous feeding and hunting ground for Herons. Beyond lay the plains and the desert.

I glided on the wind currents, wings outspread, scanning the horizon for Crows. The sky was dotted with clouds but empty of life.

As I descended, I could see that a large area of the marshes had been trampled down. This was a reassuring sign that many herons had assembled here.

Senar had commanded Stora - the head of the flocks that normally inhabited this area - to take charge of the mass migration of Herons to the West and safety.

In the next few hours I gorged myself on the abundant river fish. I didn't know how far I would have to travel on the next stage of my journey before I had another chance to eat. Sleepiness overcame me and, when I woke, the dying light of the day was disappearing and the moon was on the rise.

My Grandfather had always told me Black Crows were scared of the dark but that could not be counted on now that the traitors Matanle and Zorfar were in command. Once more I touched the Sacred Plume, firmly fixed in my chest feathers, before winging upwards into the night sky I took a bearing on the stars. We Herons have used them from time immemorial to guide us. I would also be able to follow some of the markers on the ancient migratory paths that crossed the plains. These extensive grasslands eventually led to sparse scrubland on the edge of the desert too hot to be crossed by day.

None of us had ventured beyond this point before. Migratory birds had told us to look out for the desert canyon which would provide some shade and protect flocks from the occasional harsh winds and storms that could spring up from nowhere. It contained some watering holes and I was counting on the fact that Stora would find them.

The next days and nights passed without incident. I would scout out my surroundings, flying as high as I could, looking for tell-tale tracks, markers and signs of the Heron flocks and the pursuing Crows, before resting in the shade and flying at night.

Then came the end of the day when I first caught sight, across the Western horizon, the far edge of the plain where my great nation's flocks, thousands of them, were resting before undertaking the desert journey. I would be with them soon. As I turned to look behind me to the East I shuddered. Far off in the distance was a thick black line across the sky. The Black Crows were on the move and heading in our direction.

Darkness was falling but in the twilight I could just see the rearguard of the great flock criss-crossing the sky. A small flight of herons detached themselves from the mass and were flying to meet me.

Two of the lead Herons, Stratha and his son Salla, let out a great cry of recognition. I flew alongside them as they guided me down to the ground and we exchanged information about our separate journeys.

It was dark now but the light of a three-quarter moon played on the great flock. Somewhere in their midst was my own family resting or sleeping amongst our extended family flock, safely guarded by a lonely Heron standing on watch.

As we landed, Stratha gestured to Salla to return to his own watch and, when he was out of earshot, turned to me: "It has not been easy. We are too slow. The families have many young and old and sick members. We can only fly at the pace of the slowest. We have decided to rest here overnight before leaving early in the morning."

Stora rushed over to greet us. She was surrounded by the the elders of the flocks. I raised my wings and produced the Sacred Plume. All fell silent at its sight. They knew something had happened to Senar. I let Stratha recount the tale of his death. There was consternation before Stora called for order:

"We must wait no longer. We have Pelun's warning. Let us raise the alarm and leave at once." She turned towards me: "Pelun, you have given wise counsel before. What do you think?"

"Yes" I said "by all means leave but do so calmly. Do not raise the alarm. Just tell everyone that they have rested enough and that you plan to send the sick and young off in advance.

"Tell them that the first part of journey will take them to the Grand Canyon so that they can cross much of the desert in the shade and they will be able to rest during the day when the sun is at its hottest. Then let all the families follow.

"I and Stratha will take the rearguard and stay here at the edge of the plain. When the Black Crows come, we will delay their pursuit and then join you." Everyone bowed their beaks. It was agreed.

Once more I revealed the Sacred Plume. "Stora" I said "I now entrust this to you as a badge of the authority of the Council and our nation. It must never be allowed to fall into the Black Crows' possession or that of Matanle or Zorfar. Keep it safe and show it as a symbol of the freedom we seek for all of the flock. Now, I must steal a few moments with my own family."

Stratha had shown me where to find them. They were all sleeping together. The Guard Heron greeted me enthusiastically. I explained that I would not be here for long and quickly skipped across to the makeshift nest where my beloved lay asleep.

I gently nudged Rosandris awake and gave her a love greeting. I told her my tale and she understood that I had to continue to guard the flock as it was my sacred duty. Tears were not allowed but I curled my wing around her and, for a short time, we slept safely together as we had always done.

Hardly had I closed my eyes it seemed, I was awoken by Stratha. "The dawn is coming. The young and weak are already on their way, the flocks are stirring. We have left your family to last but they must now leave."

As I looked up I could see a thousand Herons circling. This was the rearguard. Heading out across the sky were tens of thousands more, great lines of family groups, winging their way to the Grand Canyon and the unknown adventure that lay beyond.

CHAPTER VII
THE CROWS

CHAPTER VII

THE CROWS

It was mid-morning and our preparations were complete. The main flocks were long gone. Our group of warriors were scattered across the ground and well camouflaged, hidden in the scrub at the edge of the desert. Above our heads, a few scouts circled at differing heights. When the Crows were spotted we could easily spring a surprise attack. That was the plan.

What I hadn't told anyone was the sheer numbers of Crows that I had seen on the horizon. There was no point in destroying morale. We were heavily outnumbered and I doubted that we could last very long in a straight fight.

Suddenly the alarm was being sounded and there was a screech from one of the high scouts. Stratha and I stood up to see for ourselves. It was fearsome.

The black line of crows I had seen before had now formed itself into a black cloud that filled the sky and blotted out the sun. It was closing fast. "What can we hope to achieve against this?" Stratha gasped.

"We have the element of surprise", I said, "Instruct the two warrior flights to wait for the Black Crows to arrive directly above and then to launch themselves in a tight formation and fly into the crow cloud, causing as much confusion and destruction as possible. This should, at the least, delay them and give our main flock more time to escape."

Stratha nodded in salute and hurried off. I think we both knew that the likelihood of escaping alive was minimal.

When it came, the cloud of Black Crows slowly circled in a whirlpool of beating wings, many thousands of them, creating a rhythmic sound overlaid with a cacophony of chatter and croaks.
They seemed unsure of whether or not to head into the desert which stretched for miles in front of them. They were all looking inward towards the middle of this dark vortex where their leaders were in discussion.

Now was the time to act. I rose up and spread my wings and all my warriors rose with me. In the distance I could see Stratha's warriors also rise. The two flights took off simultaneously then joining up to form a powerful battering ram of Herons, all with sharp beaks pointing upwards and their talons exposed.

We had surprise on our side. The Crows let out a great cry of shock and fear matched in volume by our own war cries. We smashed into the massed ranks of the Crows. Bodies flew as we drove higher, slashing and pecking, pushing onwards and upwards towards the light. It was black all around us, a maelstrom of blood and guts.

We broke through the cloud into the sunlit sky and Stratha's warriors surfaced moments later. Both of our warrior flights were much diminished. We looked down and saw the ragged hole we had made in the crow cloud.

There was no time to lose. We joined forces, rallied our surviving fighters and set off into the sky as fast as our wings could carry us. We'd succeeded in disrupting the Crows but it would not be that long before they would rally themselves and set off in pursuit.

Fairly quickly our flight began to slow down due to the number of injured birds. We agreed we couldn't just leave them behind to be picked off by the Crows so we had to turn and fight.

With the help of Stratha, we flew up and down the flights forming the remaining warriors into a long thin line of Herons ready to fight for what they believe in and for the survival of their flock.

The giant cloud of Crows bore down on us with a fury when they saw how a relatively tiny force had caused such damage to the ranks. It seemed destined that we would all die together that day.

Suddenly, they stopped and turned. We looked on in amazement. A cry went up from Strather: "It's Fedele, look". I could not believe it.

The Crows were being attacked on both sides by the Warriors from the North who had survived in large numbers and had arrived in the nick of time to come to our aid.

The battle was won and we shouted with joy. A huge flight of Herons pursued the retreating Crows while a smaller flight came towards us. At their head I could clearly see Fedele and beside him my old friend Sibad. He had got the message through.

I reared in the air with Stratha and the others to salute our saviours with the victory cry of the warriors. Fedele and I called out to each other with our family's traditional greeting.

A little while later, when the herons returned from putting the Black Crows to flight, thousands of us were gathered, relaxing in good spirits on the edge of the desert.

I had related to Fedele all that had gone on since I'd last seen him and then Sibad, in turn, recounted his adventures with Cathe.

They also had been pursued by Black Crows that were patrolling Great Lake's shores but had managed to escape and make their way to the North in search of Fedele and the warriors.

They eventually found them hidden on the far North shore of Great Lake. Fedele's warriors welcomed them but Sibad soon discovered that they felt disoriented and disheartened by the fact that their two commanders Matanle and Zorfar had betrayed them.

Gently but persistently Sibad raised their spirits and encouraged them to see that they must put their personal feelings aside and think about the greater good and the need to save the Heron nation.

Freshly motivated, they were soon ready to fly down the Western shores of Great Lake. They then tracked the Crows across the plain, arriving in time for the decisive battle. The only sadness was that Cathe had died in the fight.

We held a ceremony that day for all the warriors lost. I said they had fought for freedom, they had not died in vain, they had passed into a better world and that we would meet them again.

Stratha called a meeting with all the leaders of our joint forces. There news was not good. Scouts he'd sent out after the battle had reported that Matanle, Zorfar and their Heron escort had been seen with the Black Crows.

"It is now clear to us all that they have been scheming for a long time to try and get control of Great Lake. On some pretence or other, they have managed to persuade the Black Crows that they could help them destroy the Herons.

"It seems", said Stratha, "that we are not to be left in peace. They are determined to kill us and rule our nation. They know that if we are allowed to get away that we will one day return for our revenge."

There was other grave news. Fedele had glimpsed further flocks of Black Crows in the far North which, he believed, may also be heading towards us. It was agreed not to tell the warriors this grim assessment of our situation. Each Captain and Leader was sworn to secrecy.

Fedele was ordered to leave immediately with a substantial number of the fleetest Herons to fly non-stop day and night until they caught up with the main flock. Stratha and the rest of the Heron forces would stay behind to guard the rear.

CHAPTER VIII
THE OASIS

CHAPTER VIII

THE OASIS

In the following days, Sibad and I spent many hours discussing what our next steps should be. It soon became clear what the priority was. We had to target Matanle and Zorfar and destroy their hold on the Black Crows. Without their leadership it is possible the Crows might abandon their pursuit. The major problem was how we were going to get to the traitors who we knew would be well-guarded and shielded by thousands of crows. Once again it was Sibad who, after many hours staring at the sky, came up with a plan.

"There may be a way. There is an oasis not far from the desert valley where our cousins the Ibis live. They are a peaceful flock and they will hide us. When the Black Crows pass over, we may be able to locate Matanle and Zorfar and attack them from behind. It will be very dangerous as we cannot take many of our warriors with us but it is all I can think of and it's worth a try."

Two of our swift Courier Herons, allocated to us by Stratha, stood by, ready for action.

"Fly to Fedele" I commanded them. "Tell him to send fifty of his strongest warriors to the oasis. Sibad will tell you how to get there. Fly separately on different tracks so even if one of you gets lost, the message will get through. The Nation's fate depends on it." The young birds saluted and, after being briefed, flew off. We watched them until they became tiny dots in the distance. A lot was riding on their success.

Later that day, Sibad and I took flight. This was the first time we had ventured across the desert which stretched out in front of us as far as the eye could see. After many hours flying, the Grand Canyon came into view and we swooped down into its shady embrace.

Over the millennia, an ancient once-powerful river had carved out this gorge in the rocks. Some small springs and rivulets were now all that remained of a once majestic waterway. As we flew, we saw signs and tracks left by the Nation's flocks who, we hoped, were a long distance in front heading for the sea.

When we came to a bend in the valley, Sibad pointed to an old tree. This was the point where we had to fly up and over the sheltering walls of the canyon and then turn right in the direction of the oasis, home of the Ibis.

When we first left the canyon's shadow, the heat was still intense and the first hour or so was exhausting. Luckily, the sun was starting to set on the horizon and, as night came on, the temperature started to fall and the moon rose, providing some light to guide our way.

We flew on steadily, each of us deep in thought when suddenly the moon itself seemed to disappear as a great crowd of birds swept down from the heavens and surrounded us. The Ibis had arrived.

These strange bald-headed birds with dark plumage and bushy feathers were nearer Sibad's size than mine. They communicated in what sounded like low belches and looked at my wingspan in amazement as if they'd never seen a Great Heron before.

Sibad took control of the situation and screeched at them in a language I had never heard before but which the Ibis seemed to recognize. Having established that we weren't a threat, they motioned for us to follow them down to the oasis.

A ring of shrubs and trees full of nests encircled a small lake. Behind it was a rock cliff with a narrow cave entrance at its base, guarded by sentries. We landed in front of it and were escorted in by a small group of these unfamiliar birds.

We entered a chamber which had a hole in the roof through which moonlight fell. Watching us from the far side of the cave was an impressive, larger-than-life figure with fine white plumage. Sibad bowed to him and spoke at length in the strange language he had used before. Whatever was said between them, it seemed all was well.

The stranger then turned to me and spoke in my own language. "You are welcome. I am Forn, the leader of the Ibis flock. I will speak your tongue as it was taught to me many moons ago by a stranded and injured heron traveler who was rescued from the harsh desert by the Ibis and stayed here for some time. He was of your race."

Another smaller figure came out from the door behind him. He saw my inquisitive gaze. "This" he said turning "is my Mother." The old Ibis bowed to us.

"I see you cannot understand why I am different." he said. "It is because the stranger who came here was my Father. He died some time ago but he was wise and left me with much of his great knowledge about your race of Herons. Sibad has explained your predicament but you can tell us more of this threat while we eat and we will see what we can do to assist you. Then you must rest ".

Food was brought to us and, in between mouthfuls, I recounted in some detail the tale of our journey and the dangers Sibad and I had experienced. As I spoke, Forn translated my words simultaneously to the Ibis group around him. When I had finished, he said "I now understand the urgency of your situation".

We need your help" I said "to bring the traitors to account. They are the ones behind this pursuit and invasion. Without them the Black Crows will lose heart. This mission is one of great danger and, for some, certain death. If we do not succeed, the Black Crows will inflict a terrible vengeance on you which I would not wish on anyone."

There was a deep hush as the group digested my words. They looked at each other. Forn spoke. "Retire and rest and we will wake you shortly. Thank you for your honesty."

Sibad was shown to a nest in the trees by the cool waters of the oasis. We were exhausted and, although my restless mind wanted to override my tired body, I realised that both of us needed to sleep.

Strange dreams haunted my mind. I saw the ghosts of those companions we had lost. Senar came to me with a warning but I couldn't hear what he was saying. Suddenly I was woken with a start. Sibad was shaking me. "Quick" he said "rouse yourself, we are summoned."

The chamber was now full of Ibis surrounding their leader, Forn. His white plumage and size clearly marked him out from the others. He clicked his beak for silence.

"We will help you" he said "for the future of your nation is our future. According to our law, we must provide you with the hospitality and assistance you seek. We live a safe and isolated life here but that doesn't mean we are not aware of what is going on beyond the edges of our domain. If the Black Crows are on the move, they will soon discover this haven and then we, like you, will be overrun. So we will join you. We are ready to fight together against evil. Tell us your plan."

There was a great cheer in response to Forn's speech. At that moment, a messenger ran in and spoke to Sibad. He turned to me with a smile. "It is the warriors we asked for. Fedele has come with them."

It was with much joy that I was reunited with my youngest son. He had brought the fifty strongest battle-hardened young Herons with him. I looked at them with pride.

Around us the oasis was a hive of activity. Forn and two hundred of his warriors were joining us. They looked tough and unafraid and seemed to relish what was about to take place. I explained to Fedele that we needed to mix our forces. "The Ibis are smaller than us but their beaks are longer than ours. Together we make a good combination"

Fedele and Forn would lead one group and Sibad and I the other. We were planning on flying south and hiding in the Grand Canyon to await the passing of the Crows. If Matanle and Zorfar were flying in their usual place at the back of the Crow cloud, a sudden surprise ambush might be possible.

CHAPTER IX

AMBUSH

CHAPTER IX

AMBUSH

By the time Sibad and I reached the canyon with our warriors, Fedele and his scouts had already assessed the situation. The main flock of our Nation, which was travelling at the pace of its slowest members, had passed this spot just the night before.

We assumed that, by now, the Black Crows would have regrouped and would be on our tail, possibly before this day was over.

As the sun rose, we secreted ourselves in two caves which the Ibis had chosen, one on either side of the canyon. Fedele and I would wait in sight of one another at the entrances to the caves.

We did not have long to wait. The sun was climbing in the clear blue sky. The canyon was silent. There was no wind. We were on full alert.
Suddenly a single Crow scout appeared, followed by a line of them. They were hovering above the Valley when, what seemed to be a solid wall of Crows, a great chattering mass, came flying along the canyon floor, filling the whole space up to its rim.

The huge noise reverberated through the caves as the army of Black Crows passed by. I hastened back, deep into the cave, to see how our band of Ibis and Heron were faring. They seemed in good spirits but then they hadn't witnessed the size of the Crow cloud.

I was suddenly filled with self doubt. My heart sank. How could we hope to succeed against such odds? This was a futile mission.

Then suddenly my anger rose and my courage returned and I found my sense of purpose I shook my mind clear of these depressing thoughts. We must defend the Heron Nation and if this means we die a warrior's death so be it.

The noise outside was abating. I crept to the cave entrance and peered out, just in time to see the end of the black wall of Crows disappearing into the distance.

Then I saw what we had hoped and waited for – a flight of Herons. Our hunch was correct. Here were Matanle, Zorfar and their followers, still far enough away from us to prepare our trap.

I called over my shoulder to Sibad "Have them ready". Across the canyon I could now see Fedele and Forn. Sibad brought a few of our speediest Herons who were going to act as a decoy. On my signal, they sped down the Valley some distance where they then hid behind a promontory of rock.

The plan was simple. On my signal, Sibad and the herons would make lots of noise from the Valley floor, as if they were injured. The traitor Herons would have to go and investigate.

As they passed the caves, Fedele's group would emerge and go on the attack. Some of our flight would provide reinforcement to this battle but our main targets were Matanle and Zorfar who must die this day.

As the raucous cries of distress the air, one of the lead Herons turned for instructions from his commander, who was at the centre of the group. About fifty of the birds peeled off to go and investigate.

When the rest came level with the caves, Fedele and Forn's emerged and attacked. Some of his henchmen came from above having found a way out of the cave and onto a ridge. The second wave met them full on at ground level.

Screams and cries rang out as the combatants fought for their lives. The traitors' flight was in confusion, reeling from the attacks. It was working. I signaled our flight to join the onslaught and this sudden influx of fresh fighters spread panic in their ranks.

Just at that moment I caught sight of Matanle, hovering at some distance from the melee, waiting to see the outcome. As I rushed towards him I saw his eyes flash as he recognized me and immediately took off in my direction.

Then out of nowhere, I was hit a great blow on my side which knocked me off course. It was Zorfar with some of henchmen, intent on killing me.
I wheeled up into the sky, regained my balance and turned to face him. I let out a huge war cry as Zorfar flew at me, talons outstretched.

We battled beak to beak, no quarter given until, distracted by the arrival of three of my Heron troops, I pierced his neck with my sharp beak. He screamed in pain and plummeted to the ground. It was a mortal blow.

I swung round to face Matanle but he had vanished. Fedele flew up. "It's all over, we have won!" Forn flew over to join us. There was blood on his talons and his plumage was in disarray. He had a tortured expression on his face. "We have lost many in this battle" he said. "Where is Matanle? Did you kill him?" I shook my beak, "We are still looking for him."

I called the surviving herons and ibis together. "We must move quickly and make sure that no-one gets away to warn the main flock of the Black Crows. We may have destroyed one of their leaders, but they are still advancing. If Matanle has got away then they will still follow him. Some of you go and search the caves."

CHAPTER X
DESPAIR

CHAPTER X

DESPAIR

It was useless. We had been searching for a few hours and still hadn't found Matanle. Meanwhile Fedele had been interrogating a few Herons that we'd captured. One of them finally admitted that Matanle had slipped away with a few trusted followers after he saw Zorfar plunge to his death.

I hastily called our surviving warriors together for a conference. "This is grave situation we find ourselves in. We must now rejoin our nation as rapidly as possible. Let's hope we can catch them up before the Crows do."

Then Forn spoke up. "There is a way" he said "to get in front of the Crows. The Grand Canyon twists its way south through the desert before veering to the West and the Sea beyond. If we fly across the desert in a direct line, there is every chance that we can reach your fellows before the Black Crows arrive. They will not travel in the dark but we can.

This was our chance. I gave the command. "We will leave some of you here to look after the wounded. The rest of us will leave immediately."

Fedele, Sibad and Forn nodded their assent and our surviving flocks of Ibis and Heron – two-thirds of the number that had set out from the oasis – took off, flying up and over the canyon wall into the full glare of the sun.

Forn was out front, defining the flight line that we would all follow. We were fortunate to have such a powerful ally. By my side was trusty Sibad and. to my left, was Fedele, my youngest son.

I thought as long as we are together, then we have a chance to succeed in protecting the Heron Nation and the values we believe are worth fighting for.

Our numbers may have been diminished which means we are certain to be outnumbered by the cloud of crows. We have been successful in disrupting their plans in the past and have killed one of their commanders but if we are to survive the next encounter, we're going to need some luck.

The moon came up. An eerie calm settled on the desert under the stars. I prayed to our spirit ancestors for strength and guidance in the task and final battle ahead.

I must have closed my eyes or dozed off on the long all-night flight because, when I came to, Forn was flying next to me. He had picked out our route in the moonlight, leading us across the desert and we had patiently followed him. I was dazzled by the first rays of sun on the horizon.

"The heat is coming" said Forn. "but we will have to fly on. It is better to fly in close formation. That way, the beat of our wings can at least provide some draught and comfort."

"I have a better idea" said Sibad, in response. "We should divide ourselves up into equal-sized groups and fly in a stack, with the birds on the top flight closely packed together so that they shadow the ones beneath. When they've had enough, they fly down to the bottom of the stack to be replaced by the next group in line. That way all the birds would get some respite."

Forn acknowledged the wisdom of this plan and so Sibad and Fedele took control, flying up and down, giving instructions, as the birds got into formation.

My group took the first turn up top of the stack and we could already feel the powerful rays beating down on us from above. From there you could see its dancing shadow on the desert floor.

As the day wore on, I periodically flew up and down the stack, encouraging everyone to persevere. There was a grim determination in all our eyes despite the atrocious conditions.

"There it is." A tremendous cry went up across the flight. We could all see, in the distance, huge flights of Herons, our whole Nation spread out on the horizon in a long line. They were still there, intact. The Black Crows were nowhere to be seen.

The heat of the desert meant nothing to us now. We raced to join our own. We had made it.

CHAPTER XI
REUNITED

CHAPTER XI

REUNITED

By the time we reached the Nation, the flocks had settled on the sand. The Nation's outriders were the first to reach us and there were screeches of delight when they recognized who we were.

Below we could see the young birds in the middle, shielded by their mothers, with the warriors keeping watch above. Stratha and Stora had flown to meet me and showed me where my beloved Rosandris was resting. How I longed to swoop down and see her but that moment of joy was interrupted by an alarm call from Forn.

I swiftly flew up to join him and he gestured to the far distance to what looked like a black serpent bursting out of the end of the canyon. The Black Crows were on our tail.

"Forn" I said "how far is the sea?". He turned towards me and gestured in the other direction. "You are almost there" he said. "Across that horizon is a strip of dunes, then cliffs and, beyond that, the sea but I'm afraid we are too late"

"Not only are the Crows ready to strike but I can feel that the great wind is heading in our direction. It blows from the North and gathers up the sand as it travels, creating a powerful sandstorm that will destroy your Nation. You must rouse them up immediately and lead them all across the sea."

I was horrified by this news but there was no time for delay. I turned to Stratha and Stora and explained the situation we now found ourselves in.

They were shocked and both looked exhausted. "We are tired" Stora said. "We've been flying a long time. The youngsters are weak and need to rest. Many of us are scared about the dangers of crossing the sea".

"Where is the Sacred Plume?" I asked. "It is here with me" said Stora. "I have kept it safe as you asked me to." I carefully took it from her and put it in my plumage. "I will lead the flock across the Sea. We will be safe. We must trust its powers to rouse the spirits of our ancestors. They will help us"

I flew down to the great flock with the Sacred Plume held in my beak for all to see. I soared over their heads and a mass of beaks pointed skywards. A huge cry went up. "Pelun will lead us" they cried.

Within minutes the whole flock rose as one and soon we were above the dunes from where we could see, for the first time, a huge expanse of sea and, on the distant horizon, the Island where safety lay.

I flew up to a high vantage point and could see the Black Crows were closing on us from behind. As I turned my head back towards the sea, a long-line of black-winged birds flew up from behind the dunes and came towards us. We were trapped. Suddenly, Forn sped ahead of me, followed by his Ibis army. It looked as though they were sacrificing themselves by plunging into the wall of birds but, in an instant, the birds parted to form a corridor to the sea.

Forn flew back towards us. "Do not fear. They will let you pass" he said. "They are our friends the Gulls. They are here to guard your flocks until you reach the sea."

We needed no second bidding. I flew to one side urging Stratha and Stora to speed ahead with the whole Heron Nation in their wake. Could it really be that, at last, we were going to make it to freedom?

As the last of the Herons flew to safety the rearguard group of Warriors and Gulls turned our attention to the Black Crows in the distance, who were assembling themselves into a cloud, preparing to attack.

Then Forn pointed with his beak. "Here comes the storm" he said "It will do the work we cannot do." Heading straight for the Crows was a huge whirlpool of sand that darkened the sky. Even from this distance we could hear the Crows' frightened cries. The storm tore into them, sucking them into its deadly embrace, wiping them out of existence.

Satisfied that the enemy had been routed, the Gulls saluted us and flew off to shelter in the cliffs until the sandstorm passes.

Forn, Sibad, myself and three warriors were to be the last to leave. I turned to say a final farewell to Forn when a dark shape came out of nowhere and suddenly there was blood flying everywhere. A giant scream came out of Forn's beak as he fell out of the sky in front of me. There was Matanle with fresh blood on his talons. He screeched defiance at me. He had murdered our saviour.

Sibad and the warriors were already preparing themselves for combat but I gestured to them to stand back. This was my battle. I faced Matanle and stared into his hate-filled eyes.

"You may have defeated the Crows" he said "but I will see you dead Pelun. I will have my revenge. For years I've plotted and planned with the Black Crows to destroy your leadership and establish myself as the head of a new order in your place.

"Matanle" I screeched, "Your treachery is at an end, your life is over and all memory of your evil deeds will be erased from history."

In a rage Matanle rushed forward, lunging at my breast, his beak ripping across my chest making the blood flow. I swept my wing across him and caught him off balance. I could feel his hot breath on mine as our talons ripped into each other.
I knew I couldn't hold out much longer and Matanle sensed my weakness. He raised his beak to deliver a death blow. With my last strength, I turned quickly, dived beneath him and twisted my talon around his throat until he screamed and I heard his neck crack. His eyes went blank, his beak dropped, and, when I let him go, his lifeless body fell like a stone.

I was exhausted. The world went black. It seemed as if the end had come for me as well. I lost consciousness.

When I came to, I found myself in flight, cocooned by the three Heron warriors who were carrying me between them. Sibad whispered in my ear "Try and move your wings, Pelun. We are nearly there."

I opened my eyes and gently tried to flap my wings. Below me I could see a huge expanse of water and an island with Herons lining the shores looking up at me.

As I slowly swept downwards I could see the distinctive figure of my beloved Rosandris. sitting on a tree top with her wings outstretched, calling to me. I landed beside her. "My love, you are badly injured but you will survive" she said. "Rest now. Our nation owes you so much."

I was so tired I could feel my eyes closing as I lay in the comfort of my lover's wings. My last thoughts before I drifted into unconsciousness were full of happiness. It had been a long journey and a hard fight but this made it all worthwhile. I vowed to myself we would reclaim Great Lake from the Invaders but that was for another day. Now there was only a deep and untroubled sleep.

Written by Duncan Hopper

Illustrations by Neeta Pederson

Edited by John May

Printed in Great
Britain
by Amazon